A Weave of Words

an Armenian tale retold by

Robert D. San Souci

illustrated by Raúl Colón

HAMPTON-BROWN

What are
the most important
skills for life?
Why?

In memory of Patricia Lomanto,
who labored tirelessly for
the cause of literacy—
"Work, and the rest shall be won."
                              —R.D.S.S.

To Estercita,
    Forever young
                  —R.C.

A Weave of Words by Robert D. San Souci, illustrated by Raúl Colón.
Published by Orchard Books/Scholastic Inc.
Text copyright © 1998 by Robert D. San Souci,
illustrations copyright © 1998 by Raúl Colón.
Reprinted by permission.

Introductions, questions, on-page glossaries, The Exchange © Hampton-Brown.

Hampton-Brown
P.O. Box 223220
Carmel, California 93922
800-333-3510
www.hampton-brown.com

Printed in the United States of America

ISBN: 0-7362-2815-2

05 06 07 08 09 10 11 12 13 14 10 9 8 7 6 5 4 3 2 1

Prince Vachagan loves Anait, but he must learn some new skills before she will marry him.

Once there was a young prince named Vachagan, the only child of King Vacha and Queen Ashken. He was handsome, bright, and **good-hearted**; but he grew up doing only **as he pleased**, never even learning to read or write. The duties of the royal court bored him. **He lived only to hunt**, and every day he rode into the mountains, dressed in simple hunting **garb**.

....

good-hearted kind
as he pleased what he liked
He lived only to hunt His favorite activity was hunting
garb clothes

One afternoon, Vachagan **reined in his horse by a spring** and watched a young woman fill her pitcher. She was the loveliest maiden he had ever seen, with her gleaming dark eyes and black silken hair.

"May I have a drink?" he asked.

She handed the jug to him, saying, "This is melted snow. Sip it slowly. You are hot and tired, and the sudden cold could harm you."

Touched by her concern and impressed by her good sense, he did as she advised. "What's your name?" he asked, handing back the pitcher.

"Anait," she replied. "I am the daughter of Aran, the weaver."

"I'd like to meet him," said Vachagan, **dismounting**. As they strolled, he delighted in Anait's quick wit and easy laugh.

reined in his horse by a spring stopped his horse by a pool of water

Touched by her concern Pleased that she cared about him

dismounting getting off his horse

When they reached the weaver's hut, old Aran welcomed his guest and unrolled a carpet, inviting him to sit.

"What a wonderful carpet!" Vachagan exclaimed. "The king himself **has none to equal this**."

Aran smiled proudly. "This was made by my daughter. She weaves like an angel. She reads and writes and **discourses** like a scholar. Truly, I am unworthy of such a treasure."

"But Father," Anait said, "*you* taught me to read and write and weave. These blessings are **beyond price**. I am **content**."

Vachagan said to Aran, "I can't read or write; I know no craft; but I *can* give Anait riches and power. I am Prince Vachagan, King Vacha's son, and I ask for your daughter's hand in marriage."

....

has none to equal this has nothing as nice as this
discourses talks
beyond price too valuable to have a price
content happy

Anait's father bowed his head and replied, "Your highness, my daughter must decide for herself."

It was then Anait spoke. "Prince Vachagan, you honor me greatly. But how can I marry a man who doesn't know how to read or write, and who can't earn a living **by his own hands**?"

"But one day I will be king!" cried Vachagan.

"Times change," Anait said. "A king may become a servant. Then what good **is past glory**?"

"If I must prove myself to you, set me a worthy task," he begged. "Ask me to slay a dragon or catch a **phoenix**."

Smiling, Anait said, "When you can read and write and show me **some handiwork of yours**, I will be satisfied."

Seeing that she would not change her mind, Vachagan left.

---

by his own hands making things

is past glory is the power that you had

phoenix magical bird

some handiwork of yours something you have made

BEFORE YOU MOVE ON...

1. **Character** What words would you use to describe Anait?

2. **Comparisons** Reread page 6. How was Anait different from Vachagan? What could she do?

LOOK AHEAD Read pages 8–11 to find out whether Vachagan learns new things.

But he could not forget Anait. She stayed sun-bright in his memory. And her words echoed through his mind, so that he no longer enjoyed his old life.

Finally he admitted, "Anait is right. I should **master** a trade." Recalling her wonderful carpet, Vachagan decided to learn to weave, as well as to read and write.

He **applied himself to** these tasks with the enthusiasm he once gave to hunting. But his fingers, which easily fit arrow to bowstring, proved clumsy with **shuttle and yarns**. As a hunter, he could easily track his quarry by reading the clues in bent grass or faint prints or scattered pebbles. Yet he often failed to **draw meaning from** the lines and curves and dots that made up the words and sentences in books.

But each time he almost gave up, the thought of Anait drew him back to his labors. Finally he mastered these skills so well that he actually began to enjoy creating colorful woven images or sampling the wisdom and pleasures of books. He even wrote poems. They always had the same subject: Anait.

....

master learn

applied himself to worked at

shuttle and yarns the tools for weaving

draw meaning from understand

At last, he wove a splendid carpet with roses **twining** around a golden tree filled with **nightingales**. This he sent by messenger to Anait with a letter he wrote himself asking her to become his wife.

Anait wrote back, "With all my heart, I **consent**."

---

twining curling
nightingales birds
consent agree

When they married, Vachagan gave Anait a black **stallion**. She learned how to ride and use a sword, saying, "A ruler must be ready to lead an army if necessary." With her help, Vachagan took on much of the **burden** of governing.

But he always saved time for his weaving. Many evenings he sat at his **loom**, while Anait read aloud to him.

---

stallion horse

burden challenge, difficulty

loom machine for weaving

BEFORE YOU MOVE ON...

1. **Cause and Effect** Why did Vachagan learn a trade and to read and write?

2. **Paraphrase** Reread page 11. What did Anait mean when she said, "A ruler must be ready to lead an army if necessary"?

LOOK AHEAD Read pages 12–17 to find out why Vachagan goes on a dangerous journey.

There is trouble in the land. Vachagan leaves the palace and rides toward danger.

After several years, the old king and queen died, and Vachagan and Anait became king and queen. One day Vachagan **confided to** his wife, "There are reports of trouble in the east. But when I send soldiers to investigate, the people say nothing."

Anait said, "Soldiers may frighten them. Perhaps you should go yourself, dressed as a hunter, as on the day we met. If the people think **you are one of them**, they may talk openly."

"An excellent idea!" her husband said. "But you will have the challenge of ruling alone while I am gone."

"My shoulders are strong," she answered. "Take care, my love: the eastern mountains are **desolate** and dangerous."

"I promise I will return to you," he replied. And that night Vachagan set out disguised as a hunter.

....

confided to secretly told
you are one of them you are like them
desolate empty, lonely

After several days, Vachagan reached a village near the eastern mountains. There he met a merchant who asked, "Where are you **bound**?"

"Eastward," said Vachagan, "but I have heard rumors that it is risky to travel there."

"The king's men came asking questions, and anyone who spoke to them vanished," said the merchant, lowering his voice. "I warn you: stay away from the **caravan** that journeys east at dawn. No one who goes with it returns."

Vachagan thanked the man; but he **made up his mind** to seek out the caravan master. Here, the king guessed, was a clue to the mystery he hoped to solve. The next morning he paid the master—a rough-looking **scoundrel**—to join the caravan traveling east.

---

bound going
caravan group of people
made up his mind decided
scoundrel criminal; bad person

After a hard day's travel, the caravan stopped at a lonely *khan*, an inn, built into a mountainside. The innkeeper welcomed them **heartily**; but Vachagan saw a **sly** smile pass between the man and the caravan master. Vachagan laid his hand lightly on his sword hilt. He and his fellow travelers found themselves in a tunnel cut into the mountain as the innkeeper slammed and locked the iron gate behind them.

"Follow me," the man said, holding up a lamp.

They walked for a long time; finally they entered a **vast, torchlit cavern**.

---

heartily warmly

sly sneaky

vast, torchlit cavern huge cave lighted with flaming torches

BEFORE YOU MOVE ON...

1. **Cause and Effect** Why did Vachagan leave Anait and travel east?

2. **Foreshadowing** Reread page 16. How do you know that something bad might happen in the *khan*? Give two clues.

LOOK AHEAD Read pages 18–23 to find out more about the cavern.

63 2 05
Lunch number

Instantly they were surrounded. From the shadows stepped a *dev*, a creature so horrible that even Vachagan could barely look at him. The **ogre** was as big as three men, and his three heads had blazing eyes and sharp red teeth.

Instantly they were surrounded. Suddenly a lot of creatures were around them.

ogre monster

Vachagan saw that the cave was filled with chained men. He **drew** his sword; but the *dev's* followers quickly **disarmed him**.

drew took out
disarmed him took away his weapon

The *dev's* left head asked one traveler, "What is your trade?"

"I am a potter," the frightened man answered.

"Good," said the middle head. **"Put him to work."**

"Put him to work." "Make him work."

"What trade?" the right head asked another man.

"**Spare me!**" said the trembling fellow. "I have no craft."

"Into the pit!" **bellowed** the middle head.

....

Spare me! Let me go!

bellowed yelled

As Vachagan watched horrified, each of his companions was sent to **captivity** or death. But in his mind, a plan took shape. When his turn came, he looked straight at the *dev's* middle head and said, "I weave carpets worth a hundred pieces of gold."

"Truly?" asked the greedy *dev.*

"**Put me to the test** and see," Vachagan challenged.

"Fail, and I will throw you into the pit myself," warned the *dev.*

So Vachagan was chained to a loom and set to work.

Without day or night, the young king had no sense of how long he labored in the cave. He was given only *tawn*, yogurt mixed with water, or stale bread to eat. If he fell asleep, he was shaken awake by the *dev*, who commanded, "Hurry and finish! I will have my servant sell your cloth in the outside world. **And woe to you** if it does not **fetch** a hundred pieces of gold!"

....

captivity prison
Put me to the test Let me try it
And woe to you And too bad for you
fetch bring me

22

BEFORE YOU MOVE ON...

1. **Plot** What did Vachagan see in the cavern?

2. **Inference** Reread pages 21–22. What lesson does the story give about having a skill or a trade?

LOOK AHEAD Can Vachagan send a message for help? Read pages 24–27 to find out.

Vachagan fights for his life. He cleverly uses his skills to send a secret message to Anait.

In spite of little food, less sleep, and eye-straining gloom, Vachagan wove **a flawless carpet, mingling yarns of vermilion and blue, green and amber and gold.**

When it was finished, the **brutish** *dev* snatched it away. He peered at the carpet's unusual border, muttering, "I have never seen such patterns before."

"Those are magical charms; they are what make my work so valuable," Vachagan assured him. "But only wise Queen Anait will see its true worth."

Enflamed with greed, the *dev* ordered his most trusted servant to take the carpet to the queen.

....

In spite of Even though he had

a flawless carpet, mingling yarns of vermilion and blue, green and amber and gold a perfect carpet of red, blue, green, and gold yarn

brutish mean, cruel

Without word from Vachagan, Anait had grown anxious. One day, she was told that a stranger had come **bearing a rare treasure** that he would show only to her. Eager to take her mind off her fears, Anait ordered the man brought before her.

"I have come a long way to show this to you," the stranger said, unrolling a carpet before her throne.

Anait could not recall when she had seen such fine workmanship. Then her heart caught in her throat. At the center of the carpet was a golden tree filled with nightingales and circled with roses—the same pattern Vachagan had woven to **win her hand**. Wonderingly, she studied the carpet's **curious** border until she suddenly realized that the fanciful lines and swirls were really words:

> *My beloved Anait, I am the prisoner of a wicked* dev. *Whoever*
> *brings this carpet is one of my jailers. He will lead you to me.*
> *Ever your Vachagan.*

"Does the carpet please your majesty?" asked the *dev's* servant eagerly.

"Indeed!" replied Anait. "Moments ago, I was **grieving**. Now that I have seen this, I am filled with hope." Then she commanded, "Guards! Arrest this man!"

Anait **assembled her soldiers without delay**. Astride her stallion, with raised sword she cried, "We ride to save King Vachagan!"

---

bearing a rare treasure with a wonderful object

win her hand get her to marry him

curious odd, unusual

grieving sad

assembled her soldiers without delay quickly called
her army

BEFORE YOU MOVE ON...

1. **Summarize** How did Vachagan convince the *dev* to send his message to Anait?

2. **Character** Reread page 26. Did Anait act the way you expected her to? Why or why not?

LOOK AHEAD Read pages 28–32 to see what happens when Anait finds the *dev*.

Guided by the *dev's* **lackey**, they quickly reached the mountainside *khan*. At Anait's command, the soldiers broke down the iron doors; the *dev's* guards rushed out to battle. The fighting was fierce, and none fought more bravely than the queen. Time and again she **rallied** her troops and led them forward.

Suddenly, the three-headed red *dev* himself burst through the shattered doors. Though her men retreated, Anait boldly faced the monster, **brandishing** her sword.

....

lackey servant
rallied encouraged
brandishing waving

Seeing **a lone woman**, the ogre's heads roared with laughter. Once, twice, three times the creature whirled his club above his heads; then he **hurled** it at Anait's horse. But Anait **caused her steed to** leap at just the right moment, so that the club passed harmlessly beneath them.

....

a lone woman only one woman
hurled threw
caused her steed to made her horse

Then Anait **charged**. One powerful **stroke** of her sword sent the *dev's* left head flying all the way to Aleppo. A second stroke sent the right head as far as Chin-ma-Chin. And with a third, the middle head was spinning toward the top of Mount Ararat. At this, the *dev's* men **fled**.

....

charged rode toward the *dev*

stroke slice, movement

fled ran away

31

Dismounting, Anait rushed into the *khan*. "Vachagan!" she shouted as she ran down the tunnel.

Her heart **rejoiced** when she heard him reply.

In a moment she **struck** off his chains. Together they freed the other prisoners.

"I prayed you would come," Vachagan said.

"O Master Weaver, your skills restored my beloved to me," Anait said happily. "You can **claim** any reward in return."

"A kiss," said Vachagan. Then husband and wife gave each other as many kisses as a pomegranate has seeds.

*So they **attained** their heart's desire, and may you likewise attain yours.*

---

rejoiced was happy

struck cut

claim have

attained got

BEFORE YOU MOVE ON...

1. **Sequence** Reread page 28. What did Anait do after the *dev* came through the doors?

2. **Paraphrase** On page 32, explain the meaning of Anait's words: "O Master Weaver, your skills restored my beloved to me."